Dedicated to Bill Flannery . . .
who was never bored or boring
— L P

LITTLE TIGER PRESS
An imprint of Magi Publications
1 The Coda Centre, 189 Munster Road,
London SW6 6AW
www.littletigerpress.com

First published in Great Britain 2005

Text and illustrations copyright © Liz Pichon 2005
Liz Pichon has asserted her right to be identified as the
author and illustrator of this work under the Copyright,
Designs and Patents Act, 1988

A CIP catalogue record for this book is available
from the British Library

Printed in Singapore by Tien Wah Press Pte.

10 9 8 7 6 5 4 3 2 1

Bored Bill

Liz Pichon

LITTLE TIGER PRESS
London

Bill was bored. He wasn't just a little bit bored, he was **REALLY REALLY** bored.

Bill's owner Mrs Pickle was never bored.
She liked to keep busy **ALL** day.

Mrs Pickle loved reading,
but Bill thought reading
was boring.

Mrs Pickle adored gardening.
Bill thought gardening was
very dull indeed.

Mrs Pickle was a fantastic cook and a kung fu expert.
"Try this, Bill, it's fun!" she said happily.
"Oh no," sighed Bill.

Mrs Pickle also liked to do lots of cleaning.
"I'm so bored I can't even move," sighed Bill.

"Come along, Bill, let's go for
a lovely long walk," Mrs Pickle said.
"Borrrrrring," muttered Bill.
"Boring dogs get bored," said Mrs Pickle.
"Besides, it's no fun sitting around all
day doing nothing."
"I won't go," said Bill firmly.

I'm not
moving . . .

Outside the weather was dreadful.
It was cold and windy. It was so
windy that Mrs Pickle's hat flew off.
"Whoooops!" Mrs Pickle laughed.
"How borrring," groaned Bill.

Suddenly a huge gust of wind
swept down and lifted them both
off their feet.

"YIPPEEEE!" squealed
Mrs Pickle as she disappeared from
sight. Bill clung to a tree when

SNAP! the branch broke
and he was spun up into the air.

Higher and higher he went. Faster and faster, past the moon and stars and up into space he flew.

"AT LAST!" cheered Bill. "No more boring walks for me. Space will be REALLY exciting."

THUMP!

Bill landed on a strange purple planet.

The noise woke up the aliens. They all popped up to see what it was. Bill was delighted to meet them. "This planet looks like fun," he smiled. "I bet Mrs Pickle isn't having an adventure like this!"

Meanwhile, back on EARTH, Mrs Pickle gets rescued . . .

Bill asked the aliens to show him the whole planet.

"LET'S EXPLORE AND HAVE FUN!" Bill shouted.

"What's the point of exploring?" the aliens sighed.

"Exploring is borrrring."

"I'm hungry," one alien mumbled. So they all went to have some squidgy green food.

"Fantastic!" thought Bill. "Alien food MUST be delicious."

But it wasn't. The squidgy green food was **REVOLTING!** Worse still, the aliens ate it for every single meal.

Life on the planet with the aliens was not very interesting at all. They just sat around all day long doing absolutely **NOTHING.**

Bill had never been so bored.
He really missed Mrs Pickle
and her delicious food.

Bill looked at the aliens lying around the planet.
"Mrs Pickle was right!" he thought suddenly.
"Doing nothing all day is REALLY BORING!
We need to get BUSY."

"Come along!" Bill shouted to the aliens. "Boring aliens get bored. It's time to have some fun!"

It's not green!

It's not squidgy!

Bill cooked the aliens a lovely meal just like Mrs Pickle's.

He showed them some of Mrs Pickle's top kung fu moves.

Then they played some games, which everyone enjoyed.

So the aliens brought out their spaceship and flew Bill back down to earth. They all waved and said goodbye.

When Bill landed he found he was FAMOUS!

EVERYONE wanted to talk to Bill about the aliens. But the only person Bill wanted to see was . . .

. . . . MRS PICKLE!

"I'll never be bored again!" said
Bill as he hugged Mrs Pickle.

So from that day on, Bill always kept himself busy, just like Mrs Pickle did. He read books and practised kung fu.

He dug the garden and cooked delicious food.

Bill even enjoyed doing the cleaning, which Mrs Pickle thought was very helpful . . .

. . . especially when they
had so many new
friends round for tea!